Margaret Wise Brown's

Pussy Willow

edited from the original by **Diane Muldrow**

illustrated by **Jo-Ellen C. Bosson**

A GOLDEN BOOK • NEW YORK
Golden Books Publishing Company, Inc., Racine, Wisconsin 53404

First Little Golden Storybook Edition 1997   A MCMXCVII

Once there was a little pussycat not much bigger than a pussywillow. He was just as soft and gray and furry as those little flowers clinging to the branches all about him in the early Spring. So he named himself Pussy Willow.

It was a wild green world that he was born into. A forest of wildflowers grew above him. Some things were bigger than he was. Some things were smaller than he was. And he wondered at such little things.

Suddenly a bug jumped out of that wild green world and up to him.

"Where are you good to bite?" asked the bug.

"Nowhere and not at all," said Pussy Willow. He rolled the bug back in the grass with his soft fur foot.

Moonlight came. The peepers were peeping and the wildflowers were a gentle smell on the warm night air.

A little peeper peeped out of the pond.

"How do you know it's Spring?" he peeped.

"I don't," said Pussy Willow.

"When the groundhog casts his shadow
And the small birds sing
And the pussywillows happen
And the sun shines warm
And when the peepers peep
Then it is Spring."

And—splash—he was gone.

Nights passed and days passed and Pussy Willow
grew more fur.

Wild strawberries bloomed about him.

Green grasshoppers hopped over him.

Suddenly Pussy Willow looked up. His pussywillows
were gone. Gone. Little green leaves hung from the
branches where his pussywillows had been.

Where had they gone?

He would go and find them.

So off he went—

through moonlight
and
starlight

and thunder
and lightning

looking for his pussywillows.

He searched

through the day
and the night

and the wind
and the rain.

Spring passed. Along came the first butterfly and bumped bang into Pussy Willow.

"Out of my way. Out of my way," said the butterfly. "Who who are you? And what are you looking for?"

Pussy Willow sat squarely on his tail.

"Pussywillows," he said. "Did you ever see any gray fur flowers that look just like me?"

"Up in the air. Up in the air," said the butterfly. "Anything that anyone would look for is up in the air."

So Pussy Willow climbed up a tree and all around the treetops, but he never learned to fly.

One day a bee flew by. "Who are you, and where shall I sting you?"

"Don't," said Pussy Willow. "But tell me, did you ever see any gray fur flowers that look just like me?"

"Sassafras," buzzed the bee. "Look in the garden."

So Pussy Willow climbed down into a garden where he found cabbages and roses, poppies and tiger lilies.

But no pussywillows.

He went up to a big fat cabbage and asked, "Did you ever see any little gray fur flowers that look just like me?"

But the cabbage sat there in its great green silence and never said a word.

So Pussy Willow wandered through purple asters and goldenrod, through blackberries and raspberries. But still he couldn't find his lost pussywillows.

The wind began to blow. The leaves turned red and
fell from the trees. Nuts fell on Pussy Willow's head and
apples dropped about him with a loud and sudden *pop*.

Pussy Willow met a red squirrel hiding acorns.

"Are you a nut?" asked the red squirrel.

"Did you ever see a nut with whiskers and pointed ears and a switching tail?" said Pussy Willow. "I am a cat looking for pussywillows. Did you ever see any little soft gray fur flowers that look just like me?"

"Look under the leaves," said the red squirrel. "Everything that anyone would look for is always under the leaves."

The air grew colder. Snow fell. Pussy Willow hunted through snowstorms and black branches and across the shining ice. At last he fell asleep, a very tired pussycat, under a thin-branched bush. He began to dream that there was a soft purring in the air around him.

When the sun began to shine warm, a groundhog came out of the ground. And when he saw a little cat in his shadow— *Thump!*

"Get out of my shadow," he said and woke him up.

The birds began to whistle. The peepers in the pond
began to peep. It was Spring.

And when Pussy Willow uncurled himself, there
were his pussywillows. For he had fallen asleep under a
pussywillow bush and it had burst into bloom above him.

"Everything that anyone would ever look for is
usually where they find it," purred Pussy Willow.